AN AMISH COUNTRY QUARREL

RACHEL STOLTZFUS

Copyright © 2015 RACHEL STOLTZFUS

All rights reserved.

ISBN: 1522989528
ISBN-13: 978-1522989523

TABLE OF CONTENTS

ACKNOWLEDGMENTS	I
CHAPTER ONE	1
CHAPTER TWO	15
CHAPTER THREE	21
EPILOGUE	31
SIMPLE TRUTHS	37
ABOUT THE AUTHOR	47

ACKNOWLEDGMENTS

I have to thank God first and foremost for the gift of my life and the life of my family. I also have to thank my family for putting up with my crazy hours and how stressed out I can get as I approach a deadline. In addition, I must thank the ladies at Global Grafx Press for working with me to help make my books the best they can be. And last, I thank you, for taking the time to read this book. God Bless!

CHAPTER ONE

Sun bathed the light green stalks of the Rachel Troyer's family cornfield, making the bright red paint of their barn seem almost like an Englischer photograph in its vivid color. The late June air had begun to take on some of the heavy humidity of summer as best friends Rachel Troyer and Mary Schrock stood outside on the porch outside the kitchen.

It was Thursday, and the two girls were baking together as had become their habit after reaching the age of their Rumspringa a year and a half ago. Now, with two loaves in the oven and two more sets of dough rising on the counter, the girls felt they had earned a break from the growing heat. They stood, leaning against the porch railing, twin glasses of lemonade cupped in their hands.

"So, what I'm thinking, Rachel," Mary said, rocking a bit on her heels, "is when we leave Hope Crossing we'll move to Philadelphia."

"*Ya*," Rachel agreed. Her best friend Mary was always

making plans. Usually, Rachel didn't mind. Mary would chatter, her hands waving with excitement as she barreled onto one thing and then the next, but eventually she would wind down until she saw sense. Like with this leaving Hope's Crossing for her Rumspringa. She'd been talking about it for over a year, but it had been nothing more than talk and Rachel figured her friend would settle down once she found someone to court with. Someone besides Jacob who followed Mary with puppy dog eyes that glittered with something else. Not that Rachel would speak ill of Jacob. They had all known each other since they were children, it was just…Jacob had always had a way of focusing on Mary that was downright disturbing to watch.

Rachel's thoughts were cut short when she heard her best friend's next words, "Really! Gutt! I thought you'd try and talk me out of it. Soledad said she has a spare room in her apartment so as long as we can pay her for the first month—"

Rachel blinked. What had Mary been saying? Moving to Philadelphia! With a coworker they barely knew! "Wait—"

But Mary was off, her speech and hands picking up speed like a whirlwind. "I've saved up enough at the hospital, and I know you never spend anything, so we should have enough for a few months at least. We'll have to share the bed at first, but I don't mind. You don't mind, do you?"

"Sharing a bed?"

"*Ya*! We'll live in the city as *Englischers*. Go to concerts.

Dances! Throw away these boring clothes—"

"I like my clothes."

"I'm not saying you *can't* wear them. We'll need something for Christmas and to see our friend's weddings when we come home."

"It's not going to be that easy, you know."

"They can't shun us if we don't take our Kneeling Vows. We'll be able to visit."

Rachel nodded. That was true, but that didn't mean it would be *easy* to leave. Her older brother, Jebediah had left and when he'd come back the first time for Second Christmas, he'd been like a different person. Not just the hair, or the fact that he had a tattoo, but the way he talked. He said he'd imitated people on Englischer television to lose his accent, said it just made things easier. And then the following year, he'd brought an Englischer woman along who had kept smiling and telling Rachel's family how *charming* everything was: their home, their outfits, the popcorn garlands over the windows -- even the stupid chickens had been charming, though the Englischer woman had been less charmed when the rooster tried to take a good peck out of her shin.

Jeb had only stayed a couple of hours the next year, a different woman on his arm this time, who had looked over everything without saying much.

Rachel had been relieved when they'd left, a guilty feeling

she'd kept only between herself and God.

The truth was, Rachel wasn't sure she wanted to live with Englischers. She certainly didn't want to become an Englischer. They weren't bad people, but even Soledad looked at her as though she needed fixing.

Rachel tried to explain, "I'm happy here. I'm helping my mamm and daed with my baking, and we sell it to the Englischer tourists. I don't want to leave! You know your brother Thomas and I have begun seeing each other!"

"Well, I assumed you would be as ready as I am to shake loose the shackles of being Plain." Mary appeared incredulous, and Rachel's stomach sank. Mary couldn't possibly be serious! Their life was hard sometimes yes, but they didn't live in shackles. Rachel stood and started pacing away from the table they shared, more to calm her sudden anger and confusion and to physically separate herself from Mary's suggestion. "I know you've always had a restless spirit, but I didn't think you were just going to abandon us? Abandon everything that we believe in!"

"I'm not abandoning our faith! I just want to live a bigger life. You agreed with me. And Jacob's also coming. He says he's saved up enough to find a place in the city too."

"Are you sure Jacob isn't just going to be with you?"

"I know he likes me, but we're not like that! He wants to find his own place in the larger world too."

Rachel pressed her lips together. She'd warned Mary about Jacob before, how he seemed too attached to Mary, and Mary hadn't listened. As little actual interest as Mary had in Jacob, she liked the attention.

"Stop worrying about Jacob," Mary said as though Rachel's thoughts were written on her face. Which they probably were at least to Mary who had been Rachel's best friend since they were six-years-old. "The bigger question is why *can't* we have Englischer technology? We don't have to bake through the summer like rolls in the oven. We don't *have* to hire a driver when we want to go more than a few miles from our home. We can learn to drive ourselves! Lead our own lives."

"But what if I like my life here?"

Mary sighed, her lips tightening for a moment, then she said, her voice trailing off, "It's Thomas, isn't it? Maybe Thomas will want to come with us..."

Thomas was apprenticed with the Deacon's brother, a master carpenter, and showed all signs of wanting to continue in the business. He'd also made hints to Rachel about them possibly starting a home together as soon as this November, though Rachel wasn't sure she wanted to marry so quickly.

Rachel opened her mouth to try and put some of these thoughts into words, but Mary was talking again, "Let me talk to Thomas. It can't hurt to at least try, don't you think? And Rumspringa is about making a choice, but how do you make a choice if you don't know what you're giving up?"

That made sense. Too much sense. Rachel said, "*Ya*, you're right. But doesn't that mean you have to give our life a chance too? Maybe if you found someone to court with? Besides Jacob."

"I told you, I'm not courting with Jacob." Mary gave a dismissive snort, "I don't want to court with anyone here. We've known them all since we were *kinner*."

"Well, we could go to a neighboring district."

"I don't--"

"If you want me to uproot my whole life and run with you to Philadelphia, you could at least give me a chance to see if you can stay."

"You're being unreasonable!"

Rachel was being unreasonable? "I'm the only one being reasonable in this conversation!" Rachel said, her temper igniting in its usual slow burn. "How can you ask me to do something you won't even consider yourself?"

"Because you don't understand what you're asking."

"I think you should leave," Rachel said.

Mary's eyes widened. "We weren't even finished talking," she said in a small voice.

"You weren't finished talking," Rachel said. "Until you are willing to *listen*, even a little, I don't see any point to continuing this."

Mary took a deep breath. "Fine," she agreed, placing the half-finished glass of lemonade onto the railing with a nod. But there was a stubborn set to her jaw that made it clear to Rachel that her friend was far from convinced. Worse, before she turned away, she had that gleam in her brown eyes that said she was planning something.

***

Mary knew she had set herself up with a difficult task in trying to convince Thomas to leave their community, but she wasn't going to lose her best friend. Which was what leaving meant. No, she wouldn't be shunned if she left before taking her Kneeling Vows, but Mary held no illusions that if she lived an Englisch life, she would also have the freedom to pursue an Amish one. As time passed, she'd have nothing in common with Rachel at all!

No, she wasn't going to give up so easily. Nor was she going to allow her best friend to rot here in this pastoral oblivion.

Mary pulled her *kapp* back over her neatly styled hair. Her face showed her distress, but she was determined. All she had to do was convince Thomas that he'd be able to pursue a better future out of the constraints of their community, and where Thomas went, Rachel would follow.

Thomas will be able to get Rachel to see sense and change her mind.

In her brother's carpentry shop, she stood off to one side, waiting until Thomas had finished sawing a piece of lumber.

"Thomas, I need to ask you a very special favor," Mary gave him her best, innocent smile. She knew that he felt she could be manipulative; they had argued many times about her lack of humility and shame for her misbehavior in the past. He had told her bluntly that she didn't seem to know where to draw the line when it came to manipulating people to get her own way.

"What is it?" Thomas asked.

"I just had an… an argument with Rachel, and now she's—" It wasn't hard for Mary to have her voice crack with distress considering the stakes. "She's not speaking to me. Would you please talk to her and let her know how much friendship her friendship means to me? I want nothing more than to speak with her and be best friends again," Mary said. As she did, she gave him her most winsome smile, tipping her head slightly to one side.

"Are you saying that Rachel doesn't want to be your friend anymore?" Thomas looked at Mary from under thick, brown eyebrows, his green eyed gaze telegraphing his suspicion. "Something big must have happened. Rachel's a woman with a good head on her shoulders. She has a good heart, too. She wouldn't break off communication just on a whim, Mary. I'm guessing your argument had to do with one of your 'suggestions.' I'll talk to her, but I'm telling you right now – I'm much more likely to believe whatever she tells me".

"Well . . . thank you . . . I just wish you would trust your little sister more," Mary said with a little pout on her face. She left the shop and returned to the farm house where she sat thinking for a few minutes more on the situation, before rising with a sigh to start dinner. As she cut the meat and vegetables, she wore a deep, dissatisfied frown on her face.

I've always taken the lead in my friendship with Rachel. I want her to go with us —she has to go with us! Thomas will talk to her. No matter that he said he doesn't trust my side of this. I'm just . . . tired . . . of living like this! I want to be free, free to see who I want to see, do what I want to do . . . without worrying about the *Ordnung*. The sharp knife slipped on the carrot, nicking her forefinger. Releasing the knife to the cutting board with a soft, forbidden swear word, she stuck her finger in her mouth, then under cool running water.

Outside, Thomas stopped working wondering about Mary's not-so-unusual request. She always had problems in putting the needs of others above her own desires – her attempt to charm him was part of a longstanding pattern in which she would try to wheedle what she wanted out of others through surface charm. *I pray that she's just working on finding herself and her place among the Amish.*

Thomas decided he would go visit Rachel that evening – maybe she could help him figure out what was happening with Mary. After dinner, he hitched the buggy to one of his family's horses and went to Rachel's. When she greeted him, he saw that she was very troubled by what had happened with Mary.

Her dark-brown eyes were made even darker with sadness.

"Rachel, something happened today with Mary . . ." He told her what had transpired, then told her that Mary was feeling restless within the Amish community.

Rachel looked at Thomas. They had only been courting for a short time, so she didn't want to upset or offend him. She wanted, even less, to tell him just why she might have ended her long friendship with his sister. Sighing, she shook her head as she sat next to him.

"Thomas, something did happen. I don't want to say anything about it until I've prayed and thought about this. I just need the Lord's guidance to know whether I should say anything," Mary explained.

"You and Rachel have been friends ever since you were both little girls. I've lived with her as her big brother, and I am letting you know that I'm suspicious about her role in this, what her motives were. She has always tried to get her way with charm and flattery. Today was no different. I will wait until you decide you are ready to tell me what happened."

"Thank you, Thomas. I'm sorry. I wish I could have said something, but she is your sister . . ."

"*Ya.* She is. I will respect your decision and wait until you have gotten the guidance you are looking for," Thomas said. The couple shifted their attention to other, happier topics and visited until shortly before nightfall, when Thomas bade

Rachel "goodbye" and left. "I will come by again in the next day or two, depending on our work schedules," he promised.

"Thomas, thank you for understanding. If I get an answer, I'll try to let you know," said Rachel with a smile of gratitude on her gentle face.

In her room that night, Rachel bowed her head and started her conversation with God:

I am so confused. I want to stay here, and Mary wants to leave with Jacob, (and I don't even like Jacob though it's not my place to judge) even at the risk of losing our friendship. Mary went to Thomas, asking him to get me to resume our friendship. Poor Thomas is so confused and worried. He knows what Mary can be like. But until I know what You would say, I can't say anything until I know it would be appropriate. I will wait for Your answer, Lord.

Having put the issue into God's hands, Rachel went to bed, trusting that, somehow, she would get an answer. Over the next several days, she focused on other tasks – baking and providing goods for the *Englischer* tourists who came to the Hope Crossing vicinity of Lancaster. She took some time to sit on the swing and appreciate the beauty of her community, seeing the wheat and corn as it bent to the gentle breezes blowing. A few nights later, she dreamed: *She came into her parents' living room to find Thomas standing by the door with a shattered look on his face. "Thomas, what is it? What's wrong?"*

"She left. Mary left Hope Crossing. My mamm found the

note on her pillow. Mary said she had invited you and you refused. She admitted in her note that you had ended her friendship with her. Rachel, why? Why didn't you let me know? My parents – they are shattered, knowing Mary will run off and maybe never come back."

"Thomas, I'm . . . I'm sorry. I had no idea she would leave this way, or that she would do so without telling you or your parents goodbye. I never meant to hurt any of you."

"You should have said something, Rachel. I trusted you – trusted that we were developing a relationship based on honesty and respect. I see now that I was wrong. I won't be coming back to see you." He turned and left, quietly shutting the front door behind him.

"Thomas! Wait! I didn't know . . . what was the right thing . . ."

Rachel's eyes opened and she gazed around frantically, reassuring herself that she was in bed, and that it was nighttime, and that her dream of Thomas breaking off with her had not actually happened. She sat up and placed a hand over her pounding heart, swallowing quickly knowing she had just received her answer. *Thank you, Lord. Now I know what I have to do.*

After dinner the next day, she opened the front door to find a smiling Thomas standing on the front porch.

"Come in. Would you like some lemonade and cookies?"

"*Ya*, thank you." He followed her into the kitchen and, after she poured the refreshing drink, took their glasses to the front porch while she carried a small plate of homemade cookies.

"Thomas, I had a dream last night about what happened with Mary and me. In that dream, you came here and told me she had left after leaving a note for your *mamm* and *daed*. You were so unhappy with me, that I hadn't told you what happened. You told me that I had let you down by not trusting you, and then said you wouldn't be coming back. I have my answer now. I have to tell you what happened with Mary and me."

Settling herself, Rachel told Thomas the difficult story. She gulped back tears as she told him that Mary seemed disdainful of living the Plain life among her fellow Amish. She wouldn't listen to me – when I told her that I'm happy here, working with my *mamm* on baking goodies for the tourists, seeing you." Rachel took a breath and a sip of lemonade before continuing. She could see by the look on Thomas's face that she had made the correct decision.

"She got angry, asking me if my friendship with her counted for anything. She was focused only on what she thought would be 'fun,' exploring the outside world, finding jobs. I told her I couldn't support what she's planning on with Jacob. She says she'll continue the Plain life, but Thomas, I don't see how! She's planning to leave Hope Crossing with Jacob Yoder, Thomas. You need to tell your parents."

CHAPTER TWO

Thomas was stunned. He looked at Rachel with his head downcast.

"Are you sure? I know she's been restless and not happy here, but . . . this—and she wasn't even going to tell us?"

"Thomas, I'm sure. I wish I could give you a different answer . . . but I would be lying," Rachel said with sadness in her voice. "We were friends from our first day in school, and we got to be very close. Thomas, she wants to live as an *Englischer* lives –not following the Amish codes or faith. She told me that Jacob Yoder is going to leave with her, and that they are going to move to Philadelphia and get Englisch jobs like my brother Jebediah."

Hearing Rachel's sad voice, Thomas was now convinced of the seriousness of Mary's intention to leave Hope Crossing.

"I am sorry, but I need to leave. *Daed* and *mamm* need to know now, tonight. You don't know when they plan to leave?"

"Soon. That's all I know."

"Rachel, thank you. Thank you for trusting the Lord and me, enough to tell me this news. I will see you soon." He quickly grabbed her hand and squeezed it, then, before he was seen, dropped her hand. Turning, he jogged down the porch steps and ran to his buggy.

***

At the Schrock farm, Thomas found his parents and asked them to join him in the barn. "It's important."

Once inside the barn, he gave both of his parents Rachel's news. His mother was devastated and his father turned his emotions inward, as he always did.

"Thomas, you know we cannot prevent her from leaving. It is the right of her Rumspringa to leave. Who knows, she may return if she finds it too difficult."

"If she isn't killed! Englischers aren't like us!" Not to mention Jacob, who worried Thomas as much as any Englischer, not that he could pinpoint exactly why.

"Englischers are as human as we and some even as devout."

"While others are devils."

"Thomas!"

"She's my little sister! Your daughter!"

His daed sighed. "We can talk to her, but . . . you know she'll know who told you her news."

"Yes. I do. But, *daed*, she has never been happy living within our *Ordnung*."

"*Ya*, I know, Thomas. Your *mamm* and I will talk with Mary. She has two choices – learn to live within our rules or make her own way."

Thomas gripped his father's shoulder, knowing that their family's choices were few.

"*Denki*." Returning to the house, he saw Mary sitting in the living room, playing with her *kapp*.

"Goodnight, Mary," he called out to her. In his room, he got ready for bed. His parents didn't come in for another ten minutes, meaning they had discussed their family's situation privately so Mary wouldn't know they were aware of what she was planning. Thomas nodded silently to himself promising he would stay silent until the time was right to talk to her.

Mary stayed in the living room, becoming more and more frustrated with the situation and silence between her and Rachel. We're almost ready to leave and she still hasn't seen my way of thinking! I'll go talk to her tomorrow and get her to see reason. She'll be ready to leave with us when I'm done talking to her. Having reached that conclusion, Mary rose and went to her room to get ready for bed.

***

It was mid-morning before Mary was ready to drive the buggy to Rachel's parents' farm. Seeing the front door closed, she realized Rachel might not be home. She decided that her reason for her visit was too important for her to turn around without seeing if Rachel was at home.

Knocking at the door, she waited.

Inside, Rachel heard the knock on the door. Answering, she saw Mary standing on the other side of the screen door.

"Mary, if you leave you're going to change. You won't be a part of our community anymore. You will be an *outsider*! I don't think you understand what that means. My brother, who left, he hasn't been back in years, not even for the holidays. I don't want to leave. I'm happy here, happy living in the Amish faith. I told Thomas what you told me. He knows about your plans to leave. I wouldn't be surprised if your parents also know."

"You—you told them?"

"What was I supposed to do?"

Mary's lower lipped trembled, and her voice was tinged with true sadness. "Be my friend."

"When you leave, will we be friends?" Rachel asked.

Mary just stared at her.

Rachel was crying. She wiped at the tears on her cheeks with the heel of her hand. "Please, just think about it," Rachel said.

Mary nodded.

Both girls turned away, neither wanting to be left behind. Wiping tears from her face, Rachel pulled the door shut behind her and returned to the kitchen to her baking.

CHAPTER THREE

Mary, hearing that Thomas knew of her plan to leave Hope Crossing, was sure that her parents also knew. They wouldn't say anything to try and stop her, but her mamm would look at her with sad eyes full of prayer while her daed attempted to change her mind through endless lectures. Worse, she would see every moment she stayed that she had *hurt* them. Yes, Mary knew she was selfish, but she didn't want to hurt anyone. She only wanted a future, fame, and the glittering promises of phones and fake nails that she saw the tourists wear and hold with such ease.

Mary jogged back to the buggy and hurried back to Jacob's parents' farm, knowing she and Jacob would be meeting before lunchtime.

"Jacob, she told my brother about our plans to leave! Rachel. She told him. He probably already told our parents, too! She's still refusing to leave, saying she's 'happy' here, and that I should be as well."

Jacob's face darkened, stormy with his anger. He began pacing quickly back and forth, muttering to himself and thinking. "Want to leave with Mary . . . she wants Rachel to join us . . . Rachel doesn't want to leave . . . that only leaves . . ." Nodding his head twice, Jacob finally stopped pacing. "We have no choice. I'll do anything in the world for you, Mary. If you really want Rachel with you as we start our new life, she's going to have to go with us by force."

"*Nee!*"

"*Ya*! Don't worry, Mary. She'll eventually forgive you when she realizes the opportunities she has out in the world," Jacob spoke with a forced gravitas that did little to negate the hint of gleeful anticipation in his gaze. "She'll be able to do so much more than what she can do here." As he spoke, a wild, fervent light grew behind his eyes, which widened. He began pacing again, this time, moving more quickly as if propelled by something pursuing him.

Mary, hearing his words, seeing the mania in his movements, grew even more frightened. Yes, she wanted Rachel to join them. She wanted her closest friend to have the same opportunities she and Jacob would soon have – but not if it meant violence and forcing Rachel to come with them against her will. Her mouth dropped open and her eyes widened. She took two steps back from Jacob, frightened by him. *Oh! I want to be free of the Ordnung, but not by doing something against Englischer law! Against God's law! Why would Jacob suggest . . . kidnapping Rachel?*

"Jacob, I'd . . . better leave. I still have so much to do before we leave . . . I need to decide what I'm taking with me and what I'm leaving behind . . . I will see you . . ." Mary quickly turned around and almost ran back to the buggy. She nearly lost her footing as she climbed in. Flicking the reins on the horse's back, she turned and left, wanting to goad the horse into a gallop. At home, after she had brushed Blackie down and put him back into his stall with a fresh scoop of food, she walked into the house, feeling troubled.

"Mary, is that you?"

"*Ya, daed*. I am back from my errand. Blackie is brushed and eating," Mary said quietly.

"Please come in here. We need to talk to you," said Mr. Schrock.

Mary walked into the family room, where she saw her parents sitting together. A new dread settling into her belly. They knew about Mary's plan to leave.

"*Kum*. Please sit," said her father.

"Thomas told us that you and Jacob Yoder are planning to leave Hope Crossing and live in the *Englischer* world. Is this true?"

"*Ya*," Mary said, resigned to the lecture and sadness even as she refused to move her gaze up from where she had her hands clasped on her lap. "We want to see if we can make a life away from Hope Crossing. I can stay with my coworker and get my teaching certificate, and Jacob will be moving to the city so it's not like I will be totally on my own.

"You know, it's going to be much more difficult for you in their world than you think."

"I'll be fine, daed," Mary said. "I've been studying, and Jacob will be with me as a friend."

"Until temptation leads him astray. Jacob isn't—"

"Jacob isn't what? You've always had a problem with him, since we were kids."

"Jacob has always had a streak in him, a temper…with God's help, I'm sure his capriciousness can be tempered by wisdom. But you are both young. And I don't believe he wants you as a friend, or as a friend alone."

"I am not going to do anything against God," Mary said. "It's my choice how I spend my Rumspringa."

"But when you're gone, it won't be easy for us to speak with you. We won't be able to help you," her father said. "What will you do without the loving arms of our community, your *family*, to help you make the best decisions?"

"I know, *daed*. I just . . . I have a hard time understanding why we have to be bound so strictly by the *Ordnung*. I mean, we could still live simple, unadorned lives without all these rules . . ."

"My daughter, these rules remind us of the importance of

the Plain life, why we are to rely only on God. If you live outside, you'll be tempted by their technology . . . their cars, phones, televisions, computers, movies, things . . . They worship things. We worship God. Are you sure you want to leave the Amish life for . . . that?" As he said the last word, Mr. Schrock filled it with all the disdain in his body.

"I . . . I . . . want something different . . ." Mary murmured. *Do I tell them what I just learned? That Jacob's willing to commit a crime to get Rachel to go with us? What do I do?* Looking at her mother, with tears standing unshed in her eyes, Mary gulped. She held back tears of her own. "I . . . I'll be in my room, thinking . . ." She beat a hasty retreat, surreptitiously swiping a betraying tear from one cheek. This was why she hadn't wanted to talk to her parents. It was easy to make a decision when you didn't have to face the consequences of it. And her parents had been strangely prescient when it came to Jacob. She didn't want to believe that Jacob would seriously consider *violence*...violence on Mary's behalf. No! She couldn't let Jacob do that.

In her room, Mary sat on her bed, rocking back and forth, muttering to herself. "Oh, now I don't know if I want to go! If he's willing to commit a crime, I don't think I know him like I thought I did.

She would have to find a way to stop Jacob.

Should I tell Thomas? Do *mamm* and *daed* need to know this? What do I do?" Mary's face crumpled as she broke down into silent tears.

Now, she wasn't sure she wanted to leave with Jacob at all. *After all, if he's willing to commit one crime, won't he be willing to commit even more after? Maybe if I pray . . . I have learned something frightening, Lord. I want to try a new life, but not if it means I am a party to a crime. I want Rachel to be with me as we start a life away from the Ordnung. But if Jacob kidnaps her, won't I be a part of his crime? Finding out what I know now, I don't think I'll be leaving with him . . . should I tell my parents or Thomas?*

In the bathroom, she washed her face with cool water and re-combed her hair, replacing her *kapp* on her head. After helping her mother with dinner preparations, she went for a walk, choosing to walk away from the Yoder farm. Her earlier thoughts and prayer returned to her, along with something else. *You love Rachel. You would not see her come to harm. What Jacob intends to do would harm her, possibly hurting someone you say you love. You want to know if you should tell someone . . . do so. Inform your parents. Tell your brother. With their help, you can protect your friend and stop Jacob.*

Mary, hearing this as thoughts inside her, stopped suddenly. *He . . . I got my answer!* Feeling immensely relieved, she turned and returned to her parents' farm, heading straight to Thomas' carpentry shop.

"Thomas! Thomas! I need to tell you something . . . it involves Rachel . . ." Mary said, out of breath. "I was talking to Jacob earlier. We're almost ready to leave Hope Crossing, and Rachel refuses to go with us . . . and Jacob told me that we would have to make her come with us . . . against her will. That she would eventually forgive us . . . Thomas, I'm scared. I never knew that he would propose something . . . "

"Criminal?" Thomas voice came out as a low growl. He struggled with anger and fright. "Come," he said, grabbing Mary's hand. Together, they ran for the house, where Mary told them what had happened earlier.

Mary's parents and Thomas went to the Yoder farm, telling Mary to stay inside the house with the doors locked.

"*Ya*. I am too scared to open them," she said. As soon as they had left, she made sure every door and window was locked.

At the Yoder farm, her family confronted the Yoders, who summoned Jacob from the fields. In the house, they told him what they knew and asked him if it was true.

"Yes! It is! I want a different life, one that's not dictated by you or the *Ordnung*! I want to make my own decisions, find work that I like to do! Mary is to come with me, and I won't leave her or let her leave me! If that means bringing Mary's friend along as well, so be it!"

With that last alarming statement, Jacob ran out of the house and to the barn, where he saddled the horse to his buggy and drove to the Schrock farm. Jumping down from the buggy, he ran to the front door and began banging on it.

"Mary! You're in there – I know it! Why did you tell? Now all our plans are ruined!" Not getting a response, he ran to the back door.

"Mary!"

Inside the house, Mary sat on her kitchen floor, her arms snaked around her knees. The manic ferocity in Jacob's voice was terrifying as he knocked hard on the windows, shaking the glass in its panes.

"Mary, we have to go! Get Rachel!"

"No!"

"You're not going to leave me," he said. "Come on, we talked about this!"

"You can't hurt Rachel."

"You're the one who wanted her to come with us! We'll leave her. But they're after us. After me. Come on, get your stuff."

"I—" Mary's mouth went dry. She couldn't go with him, not like this. She wanted her freedom, but not in exchange for becoming a prisoner of Jacob's obsession with her.

"Where are you? In the kitchen? Come to the door, Mary. Hurry up!"

"Would you really have kidnapped Rachel?"

"I'd do anything to keep you."

Mary shivered. Though she'd known Jacob since childhood, she hadn't really *known* him.

"Mary! Get out here or I'm coming in for you!"

Mary closed her eyes, resting her forehead on her knees as she trembled. She'd never imagined herself afraid of Jacob, sweet, loving Jacob who always had time to shower her with the attention she'd wanted. Jacob, who would do anything for her, and anything *to* her, anything to keep her.

What would have happened to her if she'd gone with him?

As much as it hurt Mary to admit to herself, she hadn't thought through her escape to the Englisch world enough. She didn't know what she wanted, but she couldn't just go running off without thinking it through.

From above her head came the horrible sound of the window shattering. A rock skittered across the floor in front of her as glass rained down. Mary threw her arms over her head.

"Jacob!" Someone shouted. It was Thomas.

Dear God, thank you for saving me!

There was more shouting. "We'll hold him. Hannah, get the Bishop!" that was her daed. "Mary, are you okay?"

Mary stood, the shards of glass falling from her clothing. "I'm fine," she said and stood at the window so that her daed could see her. A trickle of blood ran down her neck, accompanied by a stinging pain where the glass had cut her."

Jacob was crying, loud, horrifying sobs as he struggled with the two larger men.

"Go with your mamm to the Bishop," Mary's daed ordered.

Mary didn't have to be asked twice. It was painful to watch Jacob struggle with her father and brother, difficult to watch the way his gaze fixed on her as though she had betrayed him.

Which Mary supposed she had, though Jacob had betrayed her first.

EPILOGUE

It was two days after Jacob's breakdown, and though gossiping was a sin, lacking any real news about what had happened to Mary and Jacob, Rachel had been forced to listen and parse what she could from the whispered rumors that had traveled faster than a wildfire from one end of Hope's Crossing to the other.

The boy went berserk.

I think Mary had to go to the hospital.

They were in it together. A robbery!

I heard someone called the Englischer police.

It was maddening, and more so because Rachel had no idea if Mary was injured or if she had runaway…or worse. Though Rachel feared she had thoroughly burned her bridges with her best friend, that didn't make her stop caring for Mary. So when Rachel's *mamm* and *daed* met with the Bishop and afterwards called Rachel downstairs with news, Rachel all but sprinted into the living room.

"*Ya, mamm*? What is it?" she asked.

"I will give you a brief explanation of what happened at your friend Mary's home," Rachel's daed began. As he laid out the situation, Rachel found herself tensing and breathing in sharply with shock as she learned what Jacob had done.

What would have happened if Mary's parents and brother not come so quickly?

Rachel's daed said, "Jacob Yoder has been sent to Green Hills for Englischer therapy. After he is released, he will stay in another community in Indiana with his uncle. He won't return. The Bishop agrees that we can't excommunicate a young man who had yet to take his vows, but we can't have him here where he might threaten you and Mary again.

Rachel nodded, accepting the wisdom of Bishop's plan. She was relieved that she would never have to see Jacob again.

"And Mary?" she asked. "Is she…also leaving?" She

prayed that Mary hadn't been sent away. Mary plan to leave had been distressing, but Rachel knew her friend hadn't meant any harm. And while Rachel had never liked Jacob, she'd never suspected him of this level of malice.

"I don't know," Rachel's daed said softly.

Later that afternoon there was a knock at Rachel's family's front door. Rachel answered the door, seeing a downcast Mary standing on the porch.

All Rachel wanted was to grab her friend and pull her into a long embrace, but before she could move, Mary said, "Rachel, can we talk, please? If you'd like, your parents can be nearby."

Rachel nodded and led Mary into the kitchen. Lemonade?"

"*Ya, denki*," Mary said. Before Rachel could even walk to the refrigerator, Mary said, "I am so sorry. I didn't know that Jacob would decide to commit a criminal act to make me happy. I have a lot to apologize for, mostly to you. I will be changing and thinking of others from now on….and, you were right. I didn't think about my decision or pray about it or anything. I just wanted to turn my back on everything without even knowing what I was turning away from. And Jacob…"

She blinked rapidly, her lashes wet with unshed tears. "I know it's too much to ask, but I'd like, sometime, if we could try and be friends again."

Rachel couldn't leave Mary standing there like that, not after all they had both been through. She closed the distance between them and took Mary's hands in hers. "I will always be your friend, no matter what you choose," she said, realizing the truth of her own words as she spoke them. She had been so worried about losing Mary to the Englischers that she had almost turned her back on their friendship before Mary had even left.

At that, Mary began to cry in earnest, her shoulders shaking. Though it wasn't the Amish way to be too demonstrative in their affections, Rachel couldn't help but bring her friend into a strong embrace. "Forever," she said. "You'll always be my best friend."

When the tears had passed, the two girls sat at Rachel's kitchen table, twin glasses of lemonade between them.

"So, you and my brother…" Mary said, a hint of her old mischief in her tremulous smile.

"Well, I haven't told you yet," Rachel smiled back, her cheeks growing pink in a deep blush. "But Thomas and I are talking about marriage. . . "

THE END.

THANK YOU FOR READING!

And thank you for supporting me as an independent author. I hope you enjoyed reading this as much as I loved writing it! I hope you enjoyed reading this as much as I enjoyed writing it! If so, you can read a sample of the next book in the next chapter.

Lastly, if you enjoyed this book and want to continue to support my writing, please leave me a review to let everyone know what you thought of my work. It's the best thing you can do to keep indie authors like me writing. (And if you find something in the book that – YIKES – makes you think it deserves less than 5-stars, drop me a line at rachelstoltzfus@familychristianbookstore.net and I'll fix it if I can.)

All the best,

RACHEL STOLTZFUS

SIMPLE TRUTHS

An Amish Country Quarrel (Living Amish) Book 2

When best friends, Mary Shrock and Rachel Troyer, are approached in the Amish market by an Englisch couple who are interested in interviewing them for an "educational" article, something seems off. And the girls find their fears well founded as the strangers embark on writing an inflammatory expose. But when one of the Englischers tries to take things beyond words, Rachel, Mary, and their entire Amish community is put in deep peril. How will this Amish community face a threat that tests their faith, family, and most of all, their innocent children? Find out in Simple Truths, Book 2 of the Lancaster County Amish Quarrel series.

CHAPTER 1

Rachel looked around her *mamm's* kitchen, shaking her head, and sighing at the mess of dishes, flour, spices, mixing and measuring spoons, and other evidence of her day of baking. She began scooping up and organizing the dishes, depositing spoons into bowls that had held batter, putting them all next to the sink. Wetting a washcloth, she wiped her work surfaces clean.

"My word, Rachel, it looks like the flour got into an argument with the milk and the spices!" Barbara Troyer quipped, smiling at her daughter.

"*Ya, mamm*, I just went straight from one recipe to the next. I'm paying for it now! Tomorrow, I'll clean in between pies, cakes and cookies." Rachel moved to wiping down the butcher-block table which had been baking-central since she started.

"How much did you get done? You have market in two days, you know." Her mother moved to the long table eyeing what Rachel had made, finishing her inspection and smiling with satisfaction. "Good! You have had a productive day today."

"Yes, thank God. I want to earn enough that I can help you and *Daed* with bills and set aside enough for savings."

"Very good. You know it's not good to build up too much debt. The less you have, the better, when Thomas asks you to marry him," Barbara ran hot water into the sink squirting dish detergent into the water to make bubbles. She busied herself washing dishes, her back to her daughter.

"*Mamm*! We've only been courting for about a year. I'm still getting to know him. Besides... after what happened with his sister's beau, I'm still getting over that," Rachel's words slowed as she remembered that frightening time, absentmindedly shaking her hand over the trash can depositing spilled flour, spices, nut shells and fruit peelings.

Thomas Schrock's younger sister Mary had been courting with Jacob Yoder. Mary had always been restless, chafing under what she viewed as the restrictions of the Ordnung. She and Jacob had come up with what was initially a harebrained scheme to leave Hope Crossing, live among the *Englischers*, find work and maintain elements of their Plain lifestyle. Mary had urged Rachel to go away with them – Rachel, not wanting to leave her Amish community or lifestyle, refused. The two got into an argument and their long friendship fractured. Jacob, obsessed with the idea of living away from the Amish community, kept pressing Mary to change Rachel's mind.

When she didn't work fast enough, he told her they would simply force Rachel to leave with them. Mary, frightened, spoke to Thomas and their parents. Mr. and Mrs. Schrock spoke to Mr. and Mrs. Yoder, Jacob's parents. Jacob became enraged and went to Rachel's so he could kidnap her himself.

The two families, along with Rachel's mamm and daed, stopped him. Because of his plans to kidnap Rachel and his actual attempt, he was sent away from the district. Mary came to Rachel and apologized for her part in the situation. Rachel forgave her old friend, and they resumed their friendship.

"*Mamm*, I'm just grateful that I don't have to be fearful of Jacob Yoder. He's getting the help he needs, and maybe he'll choose to stay with the Englischers and be happy there. It's still sad that he had to be sent away with clear instructions never to come back. It must be so hard to be cast out of your home." Rachel picked up and dried a large mixing bowl.

"*Ya,* it is sad. But, remember Rachel, he chose his path in defiance of the *Ordnung* and the Lord's will. He needs help, but we can't give it to him here."

***

Two days later, Rachel stood behind her long table selling her baked goods to the *Englischers* and tourists who came to the northern Indiana community of Elkhart. In between customers, she counted how many baked goods she had remaining – only five. Next, she counted the money she had earned, zipping the vinyl pouch back up and stashing it between the boxes she used to transport her cookies, pies and cakes.

"So, how are you doing? It looks like you're about to run out, and we still have two hours before market closes today." Mary Schrock eyed what remained on Rachel's table. Mary had remained her best friend after that dark period of last year, and Rachel was glad for their continued closeness. There had been a change in her friend; she was quieter, less the wild child of the community and more contemplative, reserved and helpful. Yes, her self-centered, me-first attitude seemed to have been replaced with a more thoughtful, caring person.

This made Rachel happy; however, the spontaneous Mary had disappeared, too. That part Rachel missed; Mary was cautious now to a fault and worried about the strangest things, like would they have enough pies to make to the close of market. Clearly, if they ran out early, the world would not explode. The *Englischers* might be a little disappointed, but they would find other things to buy until next time.

"I am doing well today." Rachel smiled at her friend making the statement more to quell Mary's nervousness than anything else. "I still have one more cake and another box of cookies," She rustled around in the last box and took them out, setting them on the long table. She shifted them so they presented attractively. "How many do you have left?"

"I'm nearly out, too. I'm glad. I need to help *Mamm* and *Daed* with bills." Mary smiled as another *Englischer* approached.

"I'd like two dozen of those brownies, please." The *Englischer* was an older woman who had been to the market before, adding, "I have a meeting, and these will go over very well. Did you make them with walnuts?"

"*Ya*, I did. Does anyone at the meeting suffer from allergies to nuts?" asked Mary as she counted out 24 brownies and carefully deposited them into a box.

"No," the woman smiled and winked at her pulling out

money to cover the purchase, "we just have several members who love nuts in their sweets."

"Great, *denki*! Enjoy them!" Smiling shyly, Mary gave the woman the box.

"Hello, miss! We would like... What kind of cake is that? Spice or peanut butter? And, oh, those chocolate chip cookies look absolutely delectable." A blonde woman walked up to the table waiting for the older woman to leave.

"This is a spice cake made with a cream cheese frosting." Rachel smiled at her two customers; one was a blonde, voluptuous woman with blue eyes, accompanied by a tall, well-built, yet slightly uncomfortable-looking gentleman with dark hair and what Rachel realized were beautiful green eyes. The woman stepped between them, commanding Rachel's attention; her bright green blouse and gray pants suit screamed of money and impropriety and her voice seemed vaguely antagonistic.

Rachel smiled again focusing her attention on the woman. She was still aware that the man was eyeing everything around him including her, from the Amish vendors in their prayer *kapps* and modest dresses to the handcrafted items and the baked goods that Rachel and Mary displayed on their tables.

"We'll take the cake and, oh, one dozen chocolate chip cookies." She seemed satisfied that Rachel was now totally attentive to her and not her partner. She pulled her wallet out of her large handbag and grinned in Rachel's direction, the rhinestones on the outer sides of the wallet flashing in the sunlight.

"Good," Rachel slid the cake into a small, deep box and placed another 12 cookies in a small box with a lid. "That will be thirteen dollars, please."

"Wow, what a bargain! We couldn't get away with this at a regular bakery." She laughed at her good fortune and Rachel thought that would be the end of it. "I have a quick question for you. How do you Amish people get along with no electricity or computers?" The woman continued to grin, her gaze expectant.

Rachel's mind stopped at the bluntness of the question. Opening and closing her mouth, she struggled for a reply that was both honest and polite. "Well, because we want to rely on God, we have chosen not to use electricity or other conveniences. We don't need electricity to get anything done."

The tall, black-haired man spoke up. "So, what do you use? Kerosene lamps? Come on, get real!" The woman shot a look of disbelief at Rachel. "You can stay close to God using a computer and electricity."

Rachel was used to these kinds of conversations which were mostly curious in nature, but the level of skepticism and mockery she was feeling left her quite uncomfortable. She was also thrown off a bit by the open, almost leering looks the man was giving her and the woman seemed overly effusive but not really friendly. She looked over at her partner then back at

Rachel. His grin and looks were not missed by his girlfriend…

THANK YOU FOR READING!

And thank you for supporting me as an independent author. I hope you enjoyed reading this as much as I loved writing it!

If so, look for this book in eBook or Paperback format at your favorite online book distributors. Also, when a series is complete, we usually put out a discounted collection. If you'd rather read the entire series at once and save a few bucks doing it, we recommend looking for the collection.

Lastly, if you enjoyed this book and want to continue to support my writing, please leave me a review to let everyone know what you thought of my work. It's the best thing you can do to keep indie authors like me writing. (And if you find something in the book that – YIKES – makes you think it deserves less than 5-stars, drop me a line at rachelstoltzfus@familychristianbookstore.net and I'll fix it if I can.)

All the best,

RACHEL STOLTZFUS

ABOUT THE AUTHOR

Rachel was born and raised in Lancaster, Pennsylvania. Being a neighbor of the Mennonite community, she started writing Amish romance fiction as a way of looking at the Amish community. She wanted to present a fair and honest representation of a love that is both romantic and sweet. She hopes her readers enjoy her efforts.

Made in the USA
Middletown, DE
11 September 2019